I'M FEELING Macaroni and Cheese

A **COLORFUL** BOOK ABOUT FEELINGS

by Tina Gallo

illustrated by Clair Rossiter

Simon Spotlight

New York   London   Toronto   Sydney   New Delhi

SIMON SPOTLIGHT

An imprint of Simon & Schuster Children's Publishing Division

1230 Avenue of the Americas, New York, New York 10020

This Simon Spotlight paperback edition August 2017

© 2017 Crayola, Easton, PA 18044-0431. Crayola®, Crayola Oval Logo®, Serpentine Design®, Macaroni and Cheese®, Razzmatazz®, Tickle Me Pink®, Purple Mountains' Majesty®, Mango Tango®, Wild Blue Yonder®, and Fuzzy Wuzzy® are registered trademarks of Crayola used under license.

Also available in a Simon Spotlight hardcover edition.

SIMON SPOTLIGHT and colophon are registered trademarks of Simon & Schuster, Inc.

For information about special discounts for bulk purchases, please contact Simon & Schuster Special Sales at 1-866-506-1949 or business@simonandschuster.com.

Manufactured in the United States of America 0717 LAK

10 9 8 7 6 5 4 3 2 1

ISBN 978-1-5344-0201-0 (hc)

ISBN 978-1-5344-0200-3 (pbk)

ISBN 978-1-5344-0202-7 (eBook)

There are so many different ways to express your feelings. You can sing a song. You can do a happy dance. You can send an emoji to a friend.
You can express your feelings through colors, too! Just turn the page to discover the magical world of expressing yourself through color.

Happy is a feeling that makes me smile.
It is a warm, bubbly, delicious color.
Happy is Macaroni and Cheese.
I'm feeling Macaroni and Cheese!
What color is happy to you?

Excited is a feeling that makes me want to jump up and down!
It is a thrilling, electrifying, dazzling color. Excited is Razzmatazz.
I'm feeling Razzmatazz!
What color is excited to you?

MYSTERIOUS...

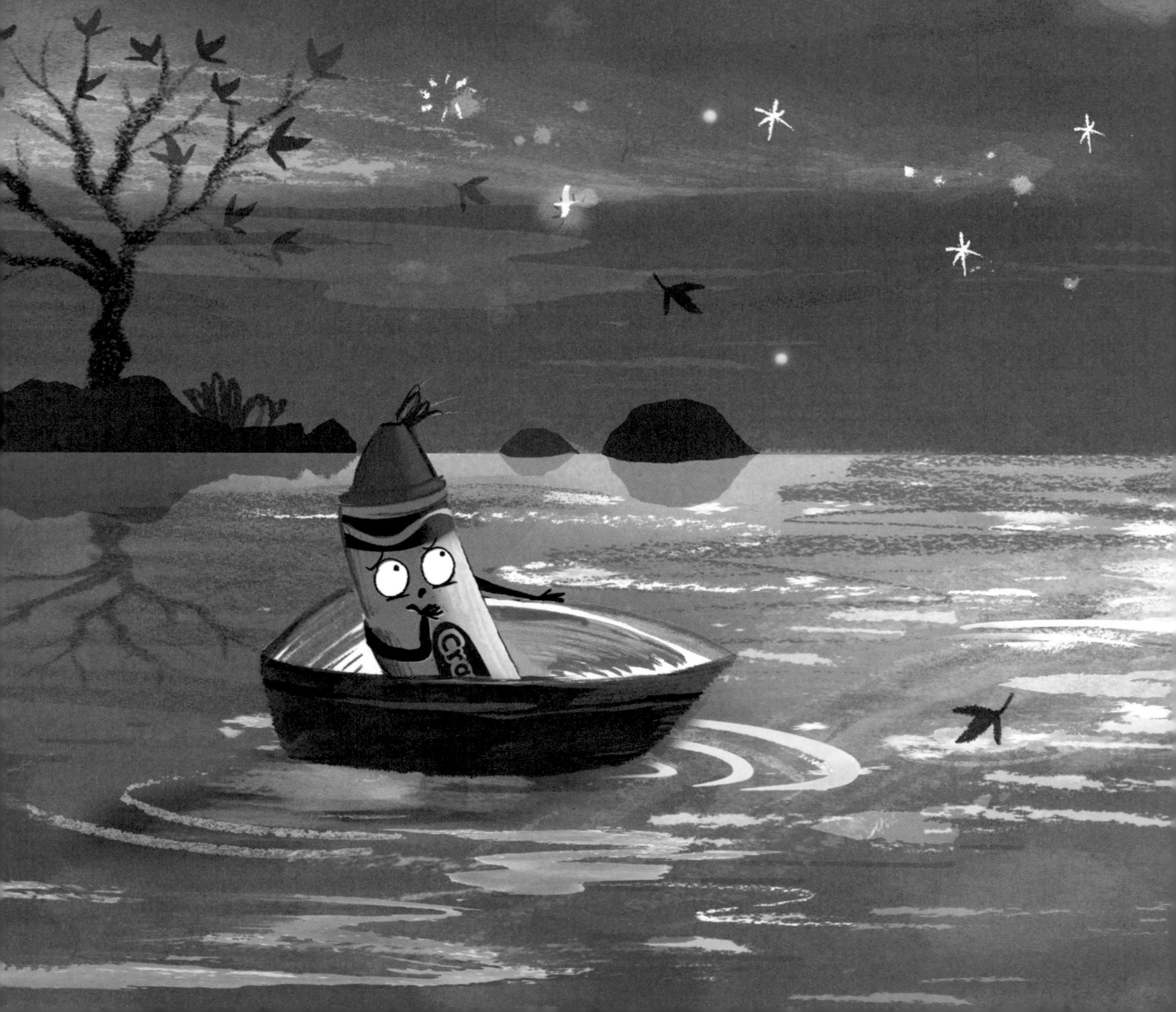

Mysterious is a feeling that makes me want to be alone with my thoughts.
It is a deep, dark, secretive color.
Mysterious is Midnight Blue.
I'm feeling Midnight Blue.
What color is mysterious to you?

Silly is a feeling that makes me laugh out loud.
It is a soft, giggly, fun-loving color.

Silly is Tickle Me Pink.
I'm feeling Tickle Me Pink!
What color is silly to you?

POWERFUL.

Powerful is a feeling that makes me stand tall and proud.
It is a rich, regal, inspiring color.

Powerful is Purple Mountains' Majesty.
I'm feeling Purple Mountains' Majesty!
What color is powerful to you?

ADVENTUROUS!

Adventurous is a feeling that makes me want to explore the world. It is a vivid, bold, fearless color.

Adventurous is Jungle Green.
I'm feeling Jungle Green!
What color is adventurous to you?

Surprised is a feeling that makes me gasp.
It is a shocking, stunning, startling color.
Surprised is Mango Tango.
I'm feeling Mango Tango!
What color is surprised to you?

COZY...

Cozy is a feeling that makes me snuggle under a blanket.

It is a cuddly, comforting, soothing color.

Cozy is Fuzzy Wuzzy.
I'm feeling Fuzzy Wuzzy.
What color is cozy to you?

Joyful is a feeling that makes me want to dance!

It is a sunny, cheerful, radiant color.
Joyful is Dandelion.
I'm feeling Dandelion!
What color is joyful to you?

Brave is a feeling that makes me want to go anywhere and do anything.

It is a daring, courageous, confident color.

Brave is Wild Blue Yonder.
I'm feeling Wild Blue Yonder!
What color is brave to you?

You can even feel different emotions at the same time.
What colors are you feeling today?
These feelings were brought to you using
the colors listed below, but you can also try
different colors. Use your imagination!

Macaroni and Cheese   Razzmatazz   Midnight Blue   Tickle Me Pink
Purple Mountains' Majesty   Jungle Green   Mango Tango
Fuzzy Wuzzy   Dandelion   Wild Blue Yonder